NO L

SEAT

D0568142

Text copyright © 2021 by Terry Farish and OD Bonny
Illustrations copyright © 2021 by Ken Daley

All rights reserved. No part of this publication may be reproduced, stored in a retrieval system or transmitted, in any form or by any means, without the prior written consent of the publisher or a license from The Canadian Copyright Licensing Agency (Access Copyright). For an Access Copyright license, visit www.accesscopyright.ca or call toll free to 1-800-893-5777.

Published in 2021 by Groundwood Books / House of Anansi Press
groundwoodbooks.com

Groundwood Books respectfully acknowledges that the land on which we operate is the Traditional Territory of many Nations, including the Anishinabeg, the Wendat and the Haudenosaunee. It is also the Treaty Lands of the Mississaugas of the Credit.

We gratefully acknowledge for their financial support of our publishing program the Canada Council for the Arts, the Ontario Arts Council and the Government of Canada.

Canada Council   Conseil des Arts
for the Arts   du Canada

ONTARIO ARTS COUNCIL
CONSEIL DES ARTS DE L'ONTARIO
an Ontario government agency
un organisme du gouvernement de l'Ontario

With the participation of the Government of Canada
Avec la participation du gouvernement du Canada   Canada

Library and Archives Canada Cataloguing in Publication
Title: A feast for Joseph / story by Terry Farish and OD Bonny ; pictures by Ken Daley.
Names: Farish, Terry, author. | Bonny, OD, author. | Daley, Ken, illustrator.
Identifiers: Canadiana (print) 20200390481 | Canadiana (ebook) 20200390554 | ISBN 9781773064383 (hardcover) | ISBN 9781773064390 (EPUB) | ISBN 9781773064437 (Kindle)
Classification: LCC PZ7.F22713 Fea 2020 | DDC j813/.54—dc23

The illustrations were created digitally in Photoshop.
Design by Michael Solomon
Printed and bound in South Korea

FSC
www.fsc.org

MIX
Paper from
responsible sources
FSC® C013572

For Ludia — TF

For Manuela and Gabriel Bonny — ODB

To my wife, Nadine — thank you for believing in me — KD

A Feast for Joseph

Story by **Terry Farish**
and **OD Bonny**

Pictures by **Ken Daley**

Groundwood Books
House of Anansi Press
Toronto / Berkeley

Joseph and Mama sit alone on the stoop of their apartment in the moon's light. People rush by.

In the refugee camp, where Joseph and Mama came from, people cooked at night in the hot wind blowing. Aunties stirred kwon and the black soot flew. Under the moon, boys played the awal.

Joseph says to Mama, "Here
there are not enough people to
eat with."

"I'm here!" Whoosh slides down the railing
from her apartment upstairs, ribbons streaming
from her whoosh of curly hair. "Now we are enough."

But Joseph is busy watching for other people.

He talks to Abuba across the ocean. "I am waiting for *you*," he says. He remembers Abuba dancing on her long legs like birds, *strut strut*.

"I have my traveling bag with good things," she says. "I wait for the waraga."

At school, Joseph scoops up the kwon and dek ngor that Mama packed for lunch. Whoosh leans over to sniff it. He offers her a taste.

"I think I might love it," she says.

When Joseph gets home from school, he looks around to see if a suitcase has come. No.

"*I'm* here!" Whoosh says.

But Joseph is calling his seven cousins and Auntie and Uncle who live across town. "When are you coming?"

Auntie says, "When we get a day off we will come."

Mama stirs kwon in a pot on the stove.

"Can I do it?" Whoosh says.

"Like this." Mama shows her how to stir with the long wooden spoon.

Joseph remembers the smell of yen burning in the cook fire. An idea begins. It begins in his belly.

The next day at school, Joseph says to his teacher, "Please come to my house. We will cook for you."

"I'd like that, Joseph," she says. "That would be fun sometime."

But his teacher doesn't come. Abuba doesn't come. No one comes.

Joseph says, "I will invite the neighbors."

"The neighbors?" Mama asks. "What if they don't like kwon and dek ngor?"

"I love kwon and dek ngor," Whoosh sings.

Joseph sees Whoosh's mami rushing by. A swish of a flowery dress.

"Come Saturday," Joseph calls out. "We will cook for you."

"You bet," she calls back. "If I don't get overtime."

On Saturday, though, everyone is too busy. No one comes.

Joseph sprawls on his back in the garden that night. Where are the people? He shuts his eyes. He tries to hear the sound of his beat on the awal. The fast tap of the wires.

Slowly Joseph picks greens from the garden plot, and yellow flowers for Mama. He will make sure they are ready when the people come.

On Sunday, a sweet smell Joseph has never known floats in, swirls around him. He sniffs. Whoosh slides down the railing.

"I'm baking a cake." She inhales the sweet air. "It takes three kinds of milk. Mami's helping."

"Cake?" Joseph says. "I think I might love it."

At dinnertime, high heels click on the stairs.
Whoosh and Mami appear at Joseph's door.
Whoosh is carrying a huge cake on a platter.

"Can we come today?" Whoosh's mami asks.

"You are most welcome," Mama says softly.

The mamas stretch their long bodies over the sofa like blossoming flowers. They start talking.

Whoosh stirs the kwon with the long wooden spoon. Joseph adds peas to the dek ngor.

Then Joseph and Whoosh carry in the kwon and dek ngor and sukuma wiki that Mama made from the greens. And flaky chapatis.

Joseph calls out, "Aii yee, Mama, a feast!"

Now the mamas lean in, eating, talking, waving
their arms, curving like the leaves of millet grass.

They all gobble and sigh.

Whoosh's mami lifts a slice of cake onto each plate. It's sweet and whipped-creamy and melts on Joseph's tongue.

Slowly a hum settles around them. A rhythm, a beat of people eating together, even if today it's only two more.

Joseph and Whoosh race outside.

"We ate and ate!" Joseph says.

"My belly's so happy," Whoosh replies.

They dance on their long legs like birds, *strut strut*, and the moon shines on the whole world, white gold.

Glossary

Abuba – An Arabic word for Grandma.

Acholi – The Acholi are people from South Sudan and northern Uganda whose language is Luo. Joseph is Acholi.

Awal – A percussion gourd of the Acholi, usually made from a pumpkin and played with a thin wire broom made from bicycle spokes.

Chapati – An unleavened flatbread common in East Africa.

Dek ngor – A traditional Acholi stew made with lentils or pigeon peas.

Kwon – The Luo word for a staple food, known by many names in many African cultures. It's a thick dough made from millet, maize or sorghum cooked in boiling water.

Sukuma wiki – A Swahili name for collard greens, kale or other greens cooked with chopped tomatoes and spices.

Waraga – An Arabic word for paper.

Yen – A Luo word for firewood.